Dear Parents,

Welcome to the Scholastic Reader ser  it
years of experience with teachers, pa
into a program that is designed to m:
and skills.

Level 1—Short sentences and stories made up of words kids
can sound out using their phonics skills and words that are
important to remember.

Level 2—Longer sentences and stories with words kids need
to know and new "big" words that they will want to know.

Level 3—From sentences to paragraphs to longer stories, these
books have large "chunks" of texts and are made up of a rich
vocabulary.

Level 4—First chapter books with more words and fewer
pictures.

It is important that children learn to read well enough to succeed
in school and beyond. Here are ideas for reading this book with
your child:

- Look at the book together. Encourage your child to read the
  title and make a prediction about the story.
- Read the book together. Encourage your child to sound out
  words when appropriate. When your child struggles, you can
  help by providing the word.
- Encourage your child to retell the story. This is a great way
  to check for comprehension.
- Have your child take the fluency test on the last page to check
  progress.

Scholastic Readers are designed to support your child's efforts
to learn how to read at every age and every stage. Enjoy
helping your child learn to read and love to read.

          —Francie Alexander
            Chief Education Officer
            Scholastic Education

To my mother Lil Carrie, and my son Damon
— G.J.

For Laura and David Kranefeld
— C.C.

Text copyright © 2000 by Garnet Jackson.
Illustrations copyright © 2000 by Carolyn Croll.
Activities copyright © 2003 Scholastic Inc.

Library of Congress Cataloging-in-Publication Data is available.

ISBN 0-439-20628-6

10 9 8 7 6 5   05 06 07
                    Printed in the U.S.A.   23
               First printing, November 2000

THE FIRST THANKSGIVING

by Garnet Jackson
Illustrated by Carolyn Croll

Scholastic Reader — Level 3

Cartwheel
·B·O·O·K·S·®

SCHOLASTIC INC.
New York   Toronto   London   Auckland   Sydney
Mexico City   New Delhi   Hong Kong   Buenos Aires

On September 6, 1620, a small, wooden ship called the *Mayflower* sailed on its way to America. It had left England with 102 people. These people came to be known as Pilgrims.

The Pilgrims had left England because King James did not want them to practice their own religion. They were in search of a new home.

Sometimes the sea was calm and gentle. The weather was warm and birds flew overhead. Fish leaped above and dipped below the clear, blue water. The children in the tiny ship laughed and played hand games.

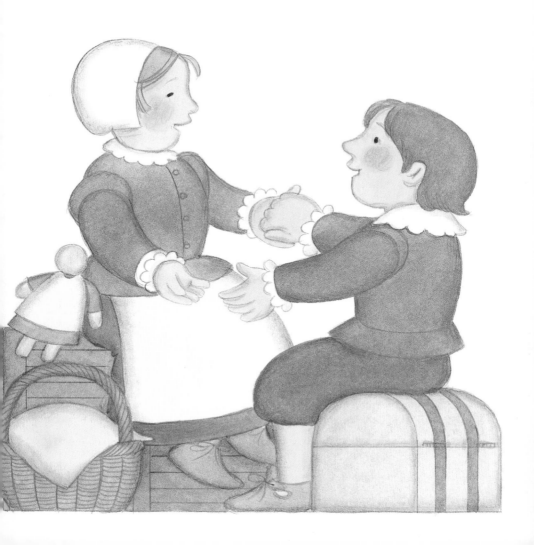

At other times the sea was rough and stormy. The sky grew gray. Large raindrops fell from the heavy clouds, plopping into the sea and into the *Mayflower*. Tall waves rocked the ship. The children were afraid.

With more gray skies than blue, the
Mayflower sailed along the ocean for two
months. Finally, after the long journey, the
weary Pilgrims sighted land.

"Land ahead!" someone shouted.

As the *Mayflower* got closer and closer, there was nothing but tall trees as far as the eye could see.

"We have found the New World!" someone said.

The Pilgrims were very happy.

Slowly, the ship made its way inland. This was December 21, 1620. The Pilgrims docked the ship and came ashore. They were on the land of the Wampanoag Nation. This was the village of Patuxet.

"We will call this new land, New England," said William Bradford, the Pilgrims's leader.

Today this place is Plymouth, Massachusetts.

The Pilgrims began to explore the new land. They saw no people. The Patuxet Wampanoag and thousands of other Native people had died from a terrible sickness that came with European fishermen in 1616.

In no time, the Pilgrims began to get settled. Winter was fast approaching. They knew they needed sturdy shelter and a place to store food. While the women took care of the children, the men began to build.

They built one big house that winter.
They called it the Common House.

The winter was bitter cold and often snowy. The Pilgrims did not have much food left from their trip. Most of the time they were hungry. They tried to stay healthy and cheerful, but it was difficult. Many of them became very sick. The Common House became a hospital for the sick. But the House did not provide enough heat to protect them from the cold, fierce winds and icy storms. Many died. Only 50 Pilgrims survived as the winter dragged on.

Then one day, the Pilgrims realized that the long, hard winter had ended. They heard birds chirping. Leaves had sprouted on the trees. Spring had arrived.

One afternoon, a Native man appeared outside. The Pilgrims were surprised when he said, "Welcome, Englishmen." He learned English from English merchants who came on ships with goods to trade. He was Samoset of the Abenaki people.

Later, Samoset brought his friend Squanto to meet the Pilgrims. Squanto knew English, too. He had been kidnapped and brought to England in 1614. Five years later, he made it back home.

Squanto taught the Pilgrims how to plant corn. He showed them how to put fish in the earth two weeks before planting. He explained that the fish would fertilize the earth and help it grow good corn.

The grateful Pilgrims began to plant corn as they were taught. They planted seeds for beans, squash, and pumpkins, too.

The Pilgrims learned how to fish,
to dig for clams, and to catch eels.

After a while, Squanto visited and brought along Chief Massasoit of the Pokanoket Wampanoag. The Chief had 60 of his men with him. They talked to the Pilgrims about why they had come to their land.

William Bradford and Chief Massasoit made a treaty. They promised to band together against people who would harm them.

Soon it was time for the Pilgrims to prepare for the coming winter. Squanto showed them how to find their way through the woods and how to hunt animals for meat.

The Pilgrims built more houses. They worked hard all summer. At the end of the summer, they had built seven small homes.

Green leaves turned red, gold, and orange
with autumn's arrival. The Pilgrims' harvest
was plentiful. There were tall stalks of corn,
large orange pumpkins, squash, and beans.
The Pilgrims were very thankful for their food.

Because they were so happy, they decided they should have a big feast and give thanks for all their blessings. That fall, in October 1621, they had a harvest feast.

For the feast, the men hunted wild turkeys that the women cooked.

Ninety Wampanoag, including Chief Massasoit, joined the Pilgrims at the feast. The guests brought deer that was cooked over a blazing fire.

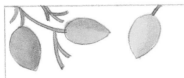

Huge servings of meat were placed on long tables that stood side by side. There were meat pies, wheat breads, and corn puddings. There were berries, grapes, dried plums, and nuts.

For three days, the Pilgrims and the Wampanoag came together in celebration — eating, dancing, and playing games.

This feast was later called the First Thanksgiving by President Abraham Lincoln. In 1863, he proclaimed the fourth Thursday of November as the official "Thanksgiving Day."